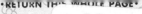

3 Great ... Mr M...

1 FREE Door Hangers and Po...

In every Mr Men and Little Miss Book like this one you...
special token. Collect 6 and we will send you either a brilliant Mr.
Men or Little Miss poster and a Mr Men or Little Miss double sided,
full colour, bedroom door hanger. Apply using the coupon overleaf,
enclosing six tokens and a 50p coin for your choice of two items.

World tokens can
be used towards any
other Egmont World /
World International token
scheme promotions.,
in early learning and
story / activity books.

Posters: Tick your preferred choice of either Mr Men ☐ or Little Miss ☐

Door Hangers: Choose from: Mr. Nosey & Mr Muddle ☐, Mr Greedy &
Mr Lazy ☐, Mr Tickle & Mr Grumpy ☐, Mr Slow & Mr Busy ☐, Mr
Messy & Mr Quiet ☐, Mr Perfect & Mr Forgetful ☐, Little Miss Fun &
Little Miss Late ☐, Little Miss Helpful & Little Miss Tidy ☐, Little Miss
Busy & Little Miss Brainy ☐, Little Miss Star & Little Miss Fun ☐.
(Please tick)

2 Mr Men Library Boxes

Keep your growing collection of Mr Men and Little Miss books in
these superb library boxes. With an integral carrying handle and
stay-closed fastener, these full colour, plastic
boxes are fantastic. They are just £5.49 each
including postage. Order overleaf.

3 Join The Club

To join the fantastic Mr Men & Little Miss
Club, check out the page overleaf NOW!

Allow 28 days for delivery. We reserve the right to change the terms of
this offer at any time but we offer a 14 day money back guarantee.
The money-back guarantee does not affect your statutory rights.
Birthday and Christmas cards are sent care of parent/guardians
in advance of the day. After 31/12/00
please call to check that the offer details are still correct.

MR MEN and LITTLE MISS™ & © 1998 Mrs. Roger Hargreaves

Join Our Club!

MR·MEN & little miss CLUB

When you become a member of the fantastic Mr Men and Little Miss Club you'll receive a personal letter from Mr Happy and Little Miss Giggles, a club badge with your name, and a superb Welcome Pack (pictured below right).

You'll also get birthday and Christmas cards from the Mr Men and Little Misses, 2 newsletters crammed with special offers, privileges and news, and a copy of the 12 page Mr Men catalogue which includes great party ideas.

If it were on sale in the shops, the Welcome Pack alone might cost around £13. But a year's membership is just £9.99 (plus 73p postage) with a 14 day money-back guarantee if you are not delighted!

HOW TO APPLY To apply for any of these three great offers, ask an adult to complete the coupon below and send it with appropriate payment and tokens (where required) to: Mr Men Offers, PO Box 7, Manchester M19 2HD. Credit card orders for Club membership ONLY by telephone, please call: 01403 242727.

To be completed by an adult

❏ 1. Please send a poster and door hanger as selected overleaf. I enclose six tokens and a 50p coin for post (coin not required if you are also taking up 2. or 3. below).

❏ 2. Please send ___ Mr Men Library case(s) and ___ Little Miss Library case(s) at £5.49 each.

❏ 3. Please enrol the following in the Mr Men & Little Miss Club at £10.72 (inc postage)

Fan's Name:_____Fan's Address:_____

_____

_____Post Code:_____Date of birth:___/___/___

Your Name:_____Your Address:_____

_____

Post Code:_____Name of parent or guardian (if not you):_____

Total amount due: £_____ (£5.49 per Library Case, £10.72 per Club membership)

❏ I enclose a cheque or postal order payable to Egmont World Limited.

❏ Please charge my MasterCard / Visa account.

Card number: [ ][ ][ ][ ][ ][ ][ ][ ][ ][ ][ ][ ][ ][ ][ ][ ]

Expiry Date: ___/___   Signature: _____

Data Protection Act: If you do **not** wish to receive other family offers from us or companies we recommend, please tick this box ❏. Offer applies to UK only

MR. GREEDY
is helpfully heavy

Original concept by Roger Hargreaves
Illustrated and written by Adam Hargreaves

MR MEN and LITTLE MISS™ & © 1998 Mrs Roger Hargreaves.
World International

Mr Greedy likes to eat.

And the more he eats the bigger he gets and the bigger he gets the heavier he becomes.

Which was a problem, as you will see.

Mr Greedy woke up and yawned and stretched.

CRACK!

BUMP!

The 'CRACK!' was the sound of Mr Greedy's bed breaking and the 'BUMP!' was the sound of Mr Greedy hitting the floor.

"Oh dear," said Mr Greedy.

Mr Greedy got up off the floor and went into the bathroom and ran a bath.

But when he got into the bath all the water got out.

There was not enough room in the bath for both Mr Greedy and the water!

"Oh dear," he said again.

Mr Greedy looked at himself in his mirror.

He had a wide mirror, but he was even wider and could not see very much of himself.

"Oh dear."

He went downstairs for breakfast.

As he waited for the bread to toast he let his hand rest on the loaf of bread.

And squashed it flat.

He even had heavy hands!

After a large breakfast of squashed toast he leant back in his chair.

There was another loud 'CRACK!' and 'BUMP!' He found himself on the floor again.

"I wish I wasn't so heavy," he sighed to himself.

Now Mr Greedy had been invited to Mr Uppity's house for lunch.

So Mr Greedy squeezed through his front door and squeezed into his car.

He started the engine.

Then, with four loud bangs, all four tyres on his car burst.

BANG! BANG! BANG! BANG!

He had to get the bus.

But when he climbed on, the other end of the bus tipped up!

"I think you need to lose some weight," suggested the bus conductor.

As the bus drove off without him, Mr Greedy looked down at his large tummy.

"Oh dear," he sighed, not for the first time that day.

Mr Greedy had to walk all the way to
Mr Uppity's house.

He was very tired and very hot and very hungry
when he got there.

Mr Uppity lived in the biggest house in Bigtown.

Mr Uppity was very rich.

Mr Uppity answered the door.

"What do you want?" he demanded.

Mr Uppity was very rude.

"You invited me for lunch," said Mr Greedy.

"Oh yes," said Mr Uppity. "You'll have to wait. I'm very busy."

"What are you doing?" asked Mr Greedy.

"Packing," answered Mr Uppity, and went up to his bedroom.

Mr Greedy followed.

Mr Uppity's bedroom was full of suitcases and every suitcase was overflowing.

Mr Uppity went round the room trying to close them, but they were so full it was impossible.

"Don't just stand there, give me a hand," ordered Mr Uppity bossily.

Mr Greedy tried pushing a suitcase shut, but it was no good.

Then he had an idea.

He sat on the lid of the suitcase and because he was so heavy the suitcase closed.

"Brilliant," said Mr Uppity. "You can shut the rest."

Mr Greedy beamed.

For the first time in a very long time Mr Greedy had found something useful that he could do.

And on his way home Mr Greedy had an idea.

An idea that meant he could be useful every day.

He went to the local newspaper and placed an advertisement.

every after. The End.

Going on Holiday?
Having trouble fitting
everything in your
suitcase?
Then call
Mr. Greedy.
The expert
suitcase squasher.

when he returned h
said what a lovely

Disaster strikes as
the daisy above M
Small's house is
blown over in high
winds.

Mr. Strong breaks
eating record by 30
eggs. Ask how he
he said 'very strong

Little Miss Bossy
fell over laughing
which is very unus

Mr Greedy had found himself a job.

He went home, ate a huge supper to celebrate, went to bed and slept.

And do you know how he slept?

I'll tell you.

He slept ...

... heavily.